Kragos & Kildor
The Two-Headed Demon

BY ADAM BLADE

ORCHARD

STORY ONE

A FIERY SECRET

My name is Taladon. Welcome to the kingdom of Avantia, which is now a place of peace, free of dark magic. The people are celebrating but in my heart I sense that the evil wizard Malvel is plotting to tear Avantia apart. Can my brave son, Tom, stop him?

A FIERY SECRET

Tom thundered along on his black stallion, Storm, with his friend Elenna behind him. His father, Taladon, rode beside him across the green hills of Avantia.

They reached a house, got down from the horses and knocked on the door. Tom's Aunt Maria answered it.

"Taladon!" Aunt Maria

cried, drawing him into a hug.
"Where have you been?"

"It's a long story," began
Taladon. "I was kidnapped
by the evil wizard, Malvel. I
escaped when Tom wounded
Malvel. He saved the Amulet of
Avantia and banished Malvel
from the country. Tom is a hero!"

"Tom! Elenna! You're safe!" Aunt Maria continued as tears welled up in her eyes. "I'm proud of you both."

Elenna settled the horses and her grey wolf, Silver, as Tom led the way out to the forge.

"Uncle Henry," he said, as he opened the door. "There's someone to see you."

Henry's mouth gaped wide. "Taladon!" he gasped. "It's wonderful to have you home."

That night, a loud crash woke Tom. He dragged on his

tunic and dashed outside to see a
huge hole in the forge door.

When Tom looked around, he
saw a golden flicker in the trees.

"What's that?" he whispered to
Elenna and Taladon, once they
had caught up with him.

Tom's heart started to thump
as a creature came into view. It
had one body, but two heads.
One of them was like a ram
while the other was like a
stag. Golden flames licked all

around, so that it stood inside a shimmering light.

The Beast gave a roar and raced away into the forest.

"Keep back, and guard the cottage!" Taladon said. He ran into the trees after the creature.

"Do you think the Beast is one of Malvel's servants, sent to hurt us?" Tom said.

Before Elenna could reply, Tom's father reappeared. He strode quickly towards the forge. There was panic and anger in his eyes.

They quickly followed and
saw him plunge one hand into
the flames of the forge. The fire
was fierce and he screwed up

his face in pain but he did not hesitate.

Uncle Henry managed to drag his brother away.

"What's going on?" Tom rushed to his father's side. "Why did you do that?"

"The Cup of Life has been stolen!" was all he could say.

"What is the Cup of Life?" Elenna asked.

"It is a magic goblet and anyone who drinks from it can repel death," said Taladon through teeth clenched in pain.

"Years ago, King Hugo gave me the cup to guard. Because it has to be kept in fire, I placed it here in the forge."

Elenna nodded. "If Malvel drinks from it he'll be strong again. And he could launch another attack on Avantia."

"The cup must be rescued. We must leave right away," Tom said to Elenna.

Taladon knew he would not be able to help his son because of his burnt hand. Aunt Maria would look after him.

Tom and Elenna mounted
Storm and set off with Silver.
On the outskirts of the forest
they heard a rustle, then
relaxed when they saw a young
deer step towards them.

"No, Silver." Elenna frowned
as the wolf growled. "He's not
dangerous."

Elenna walked beside Silver
as they went deeper into the
forest. The little deer followed a

few paces behind.

"Look there!" Elenna exclaimed at last. She pointed at some huge cloven hoof marks beside the path.

As the footprints led them deeper into the forest, Tom noticed that the trees ahead were lit up by a strange, pale silvery light.

Outlined in shimmering silver was the image of a man.

"Aduro!" Tom exclaimed. He rushed towards the vision, as he recognised the man.

It was the Wizard Aduro.
"My strength is fading," he told
them in a weak, shaky voice.
"Avantia is in great danger. You
must find the Cup of Life."

A terrible feeling of horror
and confusion hit Tom.

Aduro continued. "If the Cup of Life is not found by the next full moon, Avantia's leaders will lose their powers forever. King Hugo and I will be stranded between life and death."

"But then Malvel could take over Avantia!" Tom cried.

"The full moon is only three nights away!" Elenna added.

"The Beast's name is Kragos and Kildor," said Aduro slowly. "It has two names because it is a Beast of two natures." He waved his arms weakly. A picture of a two-headed Beast appeared in the air between them. One part was a wolf, the other a fox with cunning eyes. The image flickered and a new one appeared. This time it looked like the Beast Tom and Elenna had seen, with one

stag's head and one ram's head.

"Kragos and Kildor change their form with every generation," Aduro told them. "But whatever the form, they will always attack."

The vision of Aduro faded. Tom, Elenna and the animals followed the tracks of Kragos and Kildor. The little deer still trotted along beside them.

Gradually Tom noticed that the forest around them was changing. The ground was softer, and the air was warmer.

The trees grew even closer together and thick vines hung from the branches.

"It isn't safe to carry on. We need to make camp," Elenna said as it grew dark.

They got down from Storm's

back and Tom noticed that the little deer had disappeared.

"What's happened to our new friend?" he asked.

Tom and Elenna began to look around for the deer. Then a squeal of fear came from the darkness.

"That's him!" said Tom, and he rushed towards the sound. He chopped his way through the thick bushes until he could see the frightened animal.

At last Tom reached the place where the deer was trapped.

There were vines tangled around its legs. The deer was watching Tom and Elenna with a strange glint in its eye.

Tom swung his sword back and struck at the vine in front of him, but the ends whipped back at him.

"The vines are alive!" Tom cried out as they lunged towards him. Now he was caught in the vines. The little deer's eyes glowed with triumph.

He led me here deliberately! Tom

thought as he struggled to free himself. *But why?*

The vines dragged Tom into the undergrowth and his sword fell from his hand. When he twisted round, he saw Elenna grab it and chase after him.

"Don't give up!" she called.

Suddenly Tom saw a huge green pod. He yelled as the vines swung him up through the air and dropped him into a pool of poisonous liquid inside.

"Elenna! Help!" he cried, as sharp teeth slid from the walls and fastened onto his body. The plant was eating Tom alive.

Suddenly a sword blade stabbed through the pod and tore a hole big enough for him to clamber through.

But Tom and Elenna were

still not safe. Just then the deer
leapt into the open. Tom spun
round and saw it grow larger.
Antlers sprouted from its head
as it turned into a mighty stag.

"It's Kragos!" Elenna said.

"The little deer must have been Kragos in disguise!" said Tom. He remembered Aduro explaining that this Beast had two parts which could attack.

"Kragos and Kildor have split themselves," Tom said. "The

tracks we followed must belong to Kildor, the ram part."

"And he still has the Cup of Life," said Elenna. "We must stop him!"

"Take Storm and Silver somewhere safe," Tom whispered to Elenna.

Then Kragos charged towards Tom. He staggered back, but managed to jab his sword into into the stag's side. Kragos bellowed in pain, but then came another sound. It was the sound of a group of

hunters on horseback. Their horses crashed through the undergrowth. The hunters fired a flurry of arrows, which zipped through the air. Tom lay flat as the hunters raced after Kragos – who they thought was just an ordinary stag.

"No!" cried Tom in frustration as Kragos charged away. "I almost had him!"

Tom picked himself up and Elenna emerged from the trees. He noticed there was blood trickling down her arm.

"One of the hunters' arrows grazed me," she told him.

Tom carefully took out a talon that had been given to him by the magical firebird, Epos. It had incredible healing powers. He held the talon to

Elenna's arm, but nothing happened.

"It isn't working," Tom said sadly. He bandaged up her arm instead.

"I'll be fine," Elenna assured him as they set off again. The horses had churned up the earth and destroyed Kildor's tracks.

"We'll never be able to find him now," sighed Tom. "How will we know where to find the Cup of Life?"

As Tom spoke, a dim light appeared among the trees.

Tom could just make out the figures of Wizard Aduro and King Hugo. They both looked exhausted, their eyes dead.

"I think," whispered Tom,

"that Wizard Aduro is sending us a vision of what will happen if we fail in our Quest."

Elenna shuddered.

"He's telling us that we mustn't give up," Tom went on.

As the vision faded, Tom had an idea. He fished in his pocket and brought out his father's magical compass.

"Look!" Tom said to Elenna, pointing. "The compass says we must go to the Ruby Desert!"

STORY TWO

DESTINY IN THE DESERT

Malvel is searching for a way back to Avantia. He has sent his two-headed demon, Kragos and Kildor, to do his bidding. Now that they have the Cup of Life, Avantia is in terrible danger.

DESTINY IN THE DESERT

Tom and Elenna were riding towards the desert to search for the Cup of Life. It was very hot.

"We must find water," Tom said to Elenna, who sat behind him. They were both feeling weak now.

Tom turned Storm towards a town he remembered from a previous deadly Quest. He knew there was a well there so they could all rest and drink.

The road plunged into a deep
ravine with rock rising high up
on either side.

Tom patted his faithful
horse's neck. "Just one good
gallop, Storm," he said. "When
we get there you can have all
the water you want."

Storm raced along the rocky track. Sparks flew up from his hooves. Elenna clung tightly to Tom's waist, and Silver bounded alongside.

"Go, boy!" Tom shouted.

The end of the ravine, where the path plunged back into bright sunlight, was really close when Tom heard a rumble like distant thunder. A huge section of the cliff face had torn free. Great rocks were sliding downwards, carrying earth and trees with them.

"No!" Tom yelled. He knew there was no time to outrun the landslide. He pulled on Storm's reins with all his strength and managed to turn the horse back the way they had come.

There was a booming sound, and an avalanche of rocks crashed down. Silver was knocked off his feet but somehow managed to scramble free again.

The four friends were safe, but the road they had meant to take was now completely blocked by rocks. Tom wondered how they would get through. Then he remembered the purple jewel he had won when he defeated Sting the Scorpion Man. The jewel had the magical power to cut through rock.

Tom pulled the jewel from his belt and held it to the rocks. Purple light glowed from the gem and there was a loud creak.

Tom stared as a huge boulder began to crumble.

"It's working!" Elenna said, grinning widely.

With the power of the jewel they cleared a path through the boulders. Soon they were on their way again.

When they reached the town, they rested by the well and drank thirstily. A man leading a horse and a mule came to drink too. Tom had an important question for him.

"What's the hottest place in the desert?" he asked, remembering what his father had said. The Cup of Life had to be placed in fire before its magic

would work again.

"The Valley of Eternal
Flame," the man replied. "The
fire there never goes out."

Excitement surged through
Tom. Now they would soon get
back the Cup of Life!

The sun beat down on Tom, Elenna, Storm and Silver as they headed into the desert. Before long, the heat began to drain Elenna's strength and her eyes started to flicker.

"My arm feels worse," she said at last, sounding weak.

Tom was worried. He got down from Storm and helped Elenna down beside him. When he removed the bandage, he saw that the cut had stopped bleeding, but it had turned a deep grey colour. All around it, Elenna's arm was turning red.

"The arrow must have been poisoned," Tom said quietly. He was shocked and afraid for his friend.

"I'm strong," Elenna assured him. "I can fight it off until we return to Errinel. Aunt Maria will know what to do."

Tom was not so sure.

Suddenly, Silver gave an excited yelp. Tom saw the wolf digging at the roots of a bush with green leaves.

"He's found something," Elenna said.

"That's sagebrush!" Tom exclaimed. "Aunt Maria uses

the root to treat scrapes and scratches. Well done, Silver!"

Tom dashed over to the bush and helped the grey wolf to dig until enough sand was cleared away from the roots. Tom took out his knife and cut away a piece of the root. He used his knife to cut it open and squeezed the juices onto Elenna's wound.

Her arm didn't look any different but Elenna sighed. "That feels so much better!" she said, and gave Silver a big hug.

Tom cut some more of the sagebrush root and tucked it into his saddlebag, just in case.

"Let's go!" Tom said. "It can't be far now!"

The air grew even hotter as Tom and Elenna ventured further into the desert. At last Tom spotted a dot of light on the horizon. As they drew closer, he could see it was a patch of burning cacti.

"The heat is so great that it even sets the cacti on fire," Tom said, shocked. "We must be on

the right track."

When the sun went down, the temperature dropped and an icy wind began to blow. Elenna wanted to rest, but Tom was frightened. She was still not well, and if she went to sleep in these freezing conditions, he thought, she might never wake up.

The friends carried on. They were all tired, but Tom knew he must stay alert. Kragos and Kildor might be lurking nearby.

The moon set, leaving them to make their way by starlight. When the sun came up, waves of fierce heat rolled out to meet

them. They must be close now.

They pushed their way through a path of huge boulders. Tom gasped when he saw what lay beyond. It was a huge pit, with flames roaring up from it. Nestling in the heart of the fire was the Cup of Life.

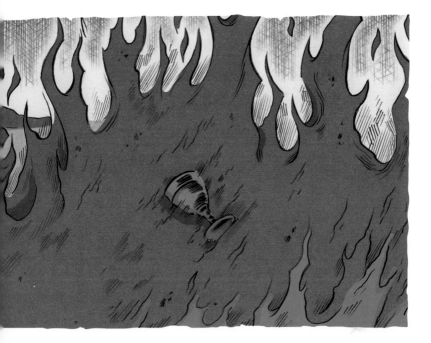

Tom had taken only one step towards the pit when he heard a great roar. A huge ram charged at him from behind another massive boulder.

"Kildor!" Tom exclaimed.

Brave Elenna fired an arrow at the creature, as the Beast reared up on his hind legs and battered Tom's shield. He lunged forwards and drove his sword into the ram's side. There was a bellowing sound and Tom saw Kragos gallop into sight. The two animals charged wildly at

each other, and their horns and
antlers clashed together.

Then the creatures' bodies melted magically into each other to form one terrifying Beast.

The Beast wore a thick leather belt studded with razor-sharp silver discs. It removed one of the discs and hurled it straight at Tom. Suddenly, there were more and more of the weapons spinning through the air. Leaping nimbly from side to side, Tom managed to dodge most of the sharp objects. Then one struck his shoulder. He felt a sharp pain and saw blood running down his arm.

Tom heard Elenna calling out. "Over here, Beast!" she said, her voice hoarse with pain.

Kragos and Kildor bellowed fiercely as they prepared to attack Elenna before she could fire her arrow.

Tom swiftly ran to meet
Kragos and Kildor as they
charged towards Elenna, then
slipped aside and began to run

around them as fast as he could. The double Beast let out a roar of anger and frustration. It turned in circles, trying to attack Tom. Soon he could see that both heads were getting dizzy. Bravely using one of Kildor's knees to help him, Tom sprang up and tumbled high over their heads. Both Beasts tried to attack him, tangling their horns and antlers horribly in the struggle. They were locked together, staggering as they tried to separate themselves.

The Beast bellowed with fury
and shook its heads. Tom saw
Elenna kneeling at the edge
of the pit of fire. She carefully
poured the last of their water
onto her handkerchief and
wrapped it around her hand to
protect herself. Then she reached

into the fire and lifted out the
Cup of Life.

Before Tom could say
anything, a roar of rage echoed
from the sky.

"It's Malvel!" Tom cried.

The roar of the defeated
wizard went on and on. Kragos
and Kildor stopped struggling.
Then Tom saw their body began
to disintegrate. Soon the twin
Beasts were no more than a
heap of sand.

Elenna held out the Cup of
Life and Tom ran towards her.

"I've got the Cup!" she exclaimed before collapsing on the ground.

Horror surged through Tom as he looked into Elenna's face. *She's dying!* he thought.

He unwrapped the damp

handkerchief from Elenna's hand. He reached for the now cooled Cup of Life, and managed to squeeze a few drops of water into it.

"Come on, Elenna," he said gently. "You must drink this, and then we have to get home. Our Quest is over."

He tilted the cup against her lips and let the few drops of water trickle into her mouth.

Slowly, Elenna opened her eyes and looked at her wounded arm. There was not even a scar!

"The Cup of Life really works!" she said, laughing with surprise.

"It really does," Tom agreed and gave a grin.

Just then, a blue light shimmered in front of them, and Wizard Aduro appeared. There was fire flashing from his fingers. Tom took a step back as the Cup of Life vanished.

"It has returned to your uncle's forge," Aduro explained. "And now you must return too."

The light flashed again. When it faded, Aduro had gone, and the desert had been replaced by the green grass of Errinel.

Tom and Elenna led the animals towards the village.

When they reached the village square, Tom and Elenna stopped, staring in surprise.

A long table heaped with
food stretched in front of them.
Many of the villagers were
seated at the table.

"Welcome home!" cried Aunt
Maria. She ran over and hugged
them close. Taladon and Uncle
Henry rushed over too, and all

the villagers started cheering.

Tom was filled with pride to think that he and Elenna had saved this happy village and the rest of Avantia from the plots of the evil wizard Malvel.

If you enjoyed this story, you may want to read

Vedra and Krimon
Twin Beasts of Avantia
EARLY READER

Here's how the story begins...

At the Royal Palace of Avantia a birthday party for King Hugo was taking place. As Tom and his friend Elenna raised their glasses in a toast, Elenna whispered in Tom's ear, "Here's to the six beasts of Avantia!"

"Shhh!" warned Tom. Most people believed the Beasts that protected the land were only a legend. But Tom and Elenna had seen them, and freed them from Malvel, an evil wizard.

The good wizard Aduro led the friends away from the party and spoke solemnly to them.

"Two new Beasts have been created," said Aduro. "They are twin dragons, and their names are Vedra and Krimon."

"Baby dragons!" gasped

Elenna, excited. But Aduro was not smiling.

"Their birth could put Avantia in danger," he said, and conjured an image on the wall. It showed the two dragons sleeping in a dark cave. One was green and the other red. Tom and Elenna gazed at the dragons, enchanted.

"Vedra is green and Krimon red," began Aduro as the vision faded. "It is rare for two Beasts to be created together. If Malvel hears about the twins, he will use them for evil purposes and harm Avantia. Will you help to protect the dragons and stop Malvel?"

"Of course we will!" promised Tom and Elenna.

READ

TO FIND OUT WHAT HAPPENS NEXT!

FREE
COLLECTOR
CARDS
INSIDE!

➤ **Series 1** ⬅

COLLECT THEM ALL!

Meet Tom, Elenna and the
first six Beasts!

978-1-84616-483-5

978-1-84616-482-8

978-1-84616-484-2

978-1-84616-486-6

978-1-84616-485-9

978-1-84616-487-3